THE NARROW WATERS

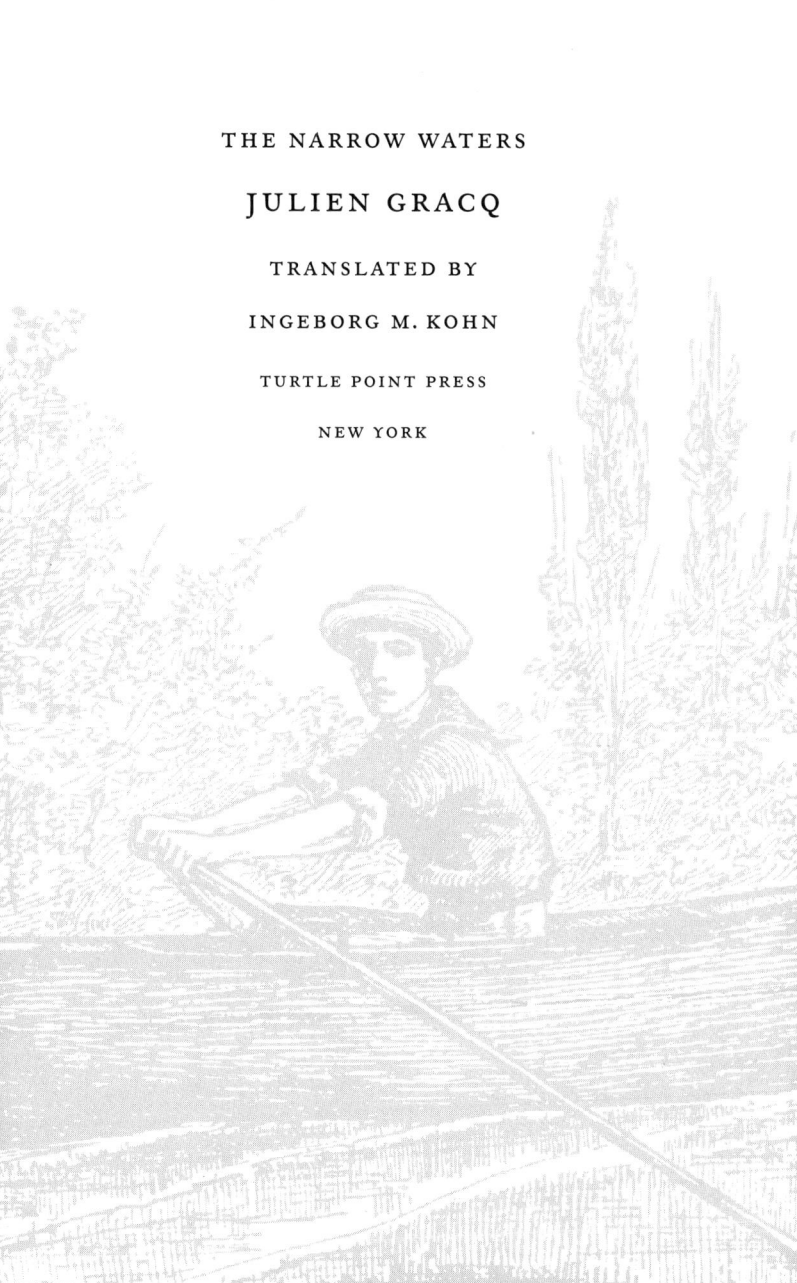

THE NARROW WATERS

JULIEN GRACQ

TRANSLATED BY

INGEBORG M. KOHN

TURTLE POINT PRESS

NEW YORK

LES EAUX ÉTROITES

COPYRIGHT © 1976 LIBRAIRIE JOSÉ CORTI

ISBN 1-885586-97-3

LCCN 2003110036

DESIGN AND COMPOSITION BY JEFF CLARK AT

WILSTED & TAYLOR PUBLISHING SERVICES

WHY DID THE FEELING ANCHOR ITSELF in me at an early age that if traveling—traveling without any thought of returning—can open doors and truly change one's life, then that most singular of all forays, an excursion with neither adventure nor unforeseen events that after a few hours finds us home again, right before the gate of our parents' house, has a more secret magic, like the handling of a divining rod? The steadfast security of return is not guaranteed to whoever risks venturing into force fields the Earth keeps charged with energy; more plausibly than does Goethe's beloved "celestial kiss," such journeys obliquely illuminate the course of our lives. At times it seems as though a grid inside us, older than ourselves, full of holes, and with entire sections missing, randomly decodes from these inspired excursions the influences that will shape future episodes in our lives. Just as an album of family photographs thumbed through by chance speaks to us of our past (a past that remains at once unspeakably personal though distinct events have been blotted out, communicating to us the vital feeling of contact with roots and the exquisite, still faintly smiling, tonality of faded things), such sites are known to mysteriously unveil the future: they already fly the colors behind which we will later rally. In contact with that earth we were somehow promised, we unfold like a Japanese flower in water: we find ourselves, inexplicably, on familiar ground, as if surrounded by the visages of a family-to-come.

Thus, the sleepy little valley of the Evre, a small, unknown tributary of the Loire about fifteen hundred meters outside Saint-Florent, encloses a privileged area in the landscape of my past more secretly, more sumptuously colored than any other—a sanctuary that remains forever attached to my earliest notions of excursion, leisure, and rural holiday. Its most singular feature seemed to be that the Evre, like certain legendary rivers of ancient Africa, had neither source nor delta that we could visit. Close to the Loire, a submerged dam made of a jumble of bulky, haphazardly dumped quarry stones, over which we could walk in the summertime toward l'Ile aux Bergères, prevented us from going upstream; a dense stand of ash, poplar, and willow encircled the network of the river's arms on the other side of the dam, discouraging any downstream exploration. Five or six kilometers upstream, at Coulènes, a mill's dam prohibited boats from continuing upstream. To go boating on the Evre also meant dealing with unavoidable formalities a day or two in advance: taking time to contact the woman who operated a café in the hamlet of Marillais to reserve the sole, ancient rowboat—rickety, dilapidated, worm-eaten, full of tar blisters, and sometimes lacking its rudder—which she kept padlocked close to the dam and allowed her customers to borrow. The handles of its mismatched oars were lodged in slings fashioned of water-willow twigs instead of oarlocks. In my memory, the sharp sensation of tangy, tepid, thirst-quenching lemonade remains inseparable from these preparations: I taste it while rereading the story of the picnic on the banks of the Cher in *Le Grand Meaulnes*. There, as in Marillais, I feel it burst against my palate with some lost, exotic reminder of bells chiming on Thursday and simple village feasts.

We used to embark—I think one still does—
at the bottom of a staircase of wooden boards that
sloped precariously down the steep clay embank-
ment; above the black waters of the narrow chan-
nel, branches grew into each other; we entered
directly into a zone of watchful, ominous silence,
a friend, like mist, of the water, broken only by
large drops falling from the blades of the raised
oars. After we pushed off, the boat was almost
immediately struck by the hollow, deep echo
from the bridge's stone arch; beyond it, the river
broadened between the low-lying meadows bor-
dered by rushes, stands of tall reeds that formed
palisades as high as the chin of the occasional
fisherman standing there as if under ambush, frozen to the spot and watchful like a sentinel. Here,
already spreading out across the river, grew the
floating green constellations of water chestnuts
that we would lift up on the return trip like a
fishing net to harvest the nuts with their sharp

protuberances: small, spiny, vegetal skulls that harden when cooked and that produce, when split, instead of a brain, a nut tasting of sugar and mud, crumbly, grainy, crunchy between the teeth.

Nothing is as surprising in my memory as the variety of miniature landscapes that border the winding river for the first few kilometers: even though the boat glides along ever so slowly in stagnant water the color of weak coffee, they seem to succeed each other with the speed of a swift, well-oiled mechanism regulating the change of stage décor, or like those Luna Park diorama panels that fold and unfold before spectators seated inside boats screwed tightly to the floor. The intense pleasure and illusion of nearly being led astray that I felt as soon as I began to read the first pages of Poe's novella *The Domain of Arnheim* were caused, I think, by the sensation of perfectly still water and the steady speed of the skiff that seems to be pulled forward by an invisible magnet rather than being carried along by a current. Years later, Lohengrin's swan moving up- and downstream on the imaginary waterways of the opera scene recalled once again, momentarily, that sensation of an almost troubling happiness, caused—something I realized only at that moment—by the impression of gradual, continuous acceleration born of such fantastical navigation. We sense that there is someone *calling out* to us with confident urgency from within those ingenious vessels—swans, skiffs, hollowed-out logs—which, in fables, traverse the surface of still water; contrary to the malevolent associations of unidentified flying objects, everlasting happiness, wish-fulfillment, or at least supernatural help when in peril, seem to spur their silent navigation.

I am speaking of Edgar Poe, who will remain with me now on this trip, which I've taken so many times before—often with loud, happy companions—and which, nevertheless, not just in my memory but every time I set out again and all the while it lasts, has always retained something dreamlike throughout that silent, incomparably majestic boat ride where the two banks approach and part like the waves of the Red Sea, leaving me with a feeling of almost unreal slowness and, at the same time, of smooth pace, which I thought I'd found again in De Quincey's most beautiful, expansive opium dreams. The "black, heavy, shadow-devouring water" described by Gaston Bachelard, the water surrounding Fairyland, the water lying in silent wait deep inside the moat, ready to engulf the ruins of the House of Usher—so different from the treacherously violent flow that grates and rakes the banks of the Loire, grabbing the swimmer by the shoulders like a big, playful dog and overturning him as he tries to steady himself—that water was right here, immediately in front of me, with its fragrance of mud and roots, its dissolving sleep: digesting, slowly steeping the leaves that would rain from autumnal trees. I never dove into it without uneasiness: it was like entering a cold, inert mass without splashing or spraying, like diving through a filmy layer of duckweed.

Once afloat on the Evre, we entered a realm removed from the rest of the earth, to which only the boat held a key. Le Chemin Vert, a weedy path, starts at the Marillais Bridge and runs several hundred meters along one of the riverbanks before coming to an abrupt stop at the edge of an uneven meadow; just beyond it, field-dividing hedgerows extend as far as the bank, to which leads no other path. Thus, when we passed in front of La Jolivière, a farm perched on a hillside high above the bank, I was always surprised that I'd been able to reach it a few times on foot, by way of a complicated network of well-worn paths, the consecrated itinerary of the long line of faithful parishioners who, every spring, followed the little bell of the Rogation procession; those steps that descend to the river from up high separated two ritual circuits of different species that should never have met. I was scandalized, as if a mystical frontier had been trespassed, to find the farm's herd of cattle stumbling down the muddy slope to drink at the river. But this was the only disenchanting trace of plowed and planted farmlands; everywhere else, the little river seemed to zig-zag across a virgin wilderness reserve, a protected area belonging to Sundays and leisure, unscarred by toil.

The Evre is scarcely more than twenty meters wide, sometimes less; its bed is deep, with several layers of river bottom in various stages of decomposition, riddled with holes and crevices in which gigantic pike hide. Today, no doubt, pollution has taken its toll there as it has on all other rivers, but in my youth a fishing expedition on the Evre meant going after big game: its licorice-colored waters, like the ponds of Fontainebleau, were known to nourish hundred-year-old fish (and, at least in my own imagination, the deep black Evre resembled that bewitched ocean in *The Manuscript Found in a Bottle,* in which everything could grow monstrously, even ships). After emerging from beneath the stone bridge in Marillais, the river spreads out between wet meadows covered with a profusion of buttercups and daisies in the springtime; alongside each bank, bouquets of reed-shafts rise in sharp points; our oars would be constantly entangled in the submerged stems and branches of water lilies and chestnuts that leave open only a narrow navigable passage. Stands of poplar still grow alongside the river; their fallen leaves blanket the October meadows, releasing a bitter, astringent smell, redolent at times of drying varnish, which for me is *the* odor of autumn in the valley. The lawns, the water lilies, the decorative, feathery reed beds on both sides of the river look almost as if they were part of a spacious park, but quotidian noise has not ceased: the trotting of a horse, echoed by the stone arch of the bridge, still reverberates in my memory, and the languid, hourly bell-tolls from the Marillais church tower (turning around in the boat, we could see its square silhouette rising above the reeds and clusters of sedge) travel for a long time over stretches of still water to catch up with you. But now the silence is no longer so easily broken, with only occasional echoes of a past that the curtain of poplars is beginning to hide. The marshlands, glimpsed just beyond the bridge, with its cackling waterhens and water bubbles made by frogs diving, are replaced momentarily by a wide plains river flowing leisurely between willows, like an untied scarf, steeped in sunlight, criss-crossed by the flights of kingfishers and dragonflies. Here and there, a narrow clearing in the reeds along the riverbank leads to two or three steps made of rotten boards; the tall fishing pole, leaning there permanently like the sign of a roadside bar, marks the spot where fishing gear, handed down from father to son, has been left in place. But these signs of watchful human presence, like alpine huts that give, from afar, the impression that a mountain is inhabited, are deceiving; while passing before the clearing, one can see that the space is empty and the fishing pole stuck in the mud; its owner, who from time to time walks from one spot to another, sometimes watches over four or five such spaces. This coastal artillery, so parsimoniously manned, does not extend beyond the end of Le Chemin Vert, which, shielded by reeds, begins to resemble a ramparts-passage traveled, from look-out to look-out, by unseen sentries; beyond it, the tension of walking alongside a patrolled minefield disappears, and with it any orders to remain silent. By now, the river has changed its course several times; the Marillais church tower has disappeared behind poplars; the low slopes that border the wet meadows are edging together, closing in. I've often walked to the end of Le Chemin Vert to picnic on the grass. Just beyond it, behind the bulge of a hill that borders the riverbank, lies another region that can be reached neither on foot nor by car, to which entry is restricted to certain lucky days: cloudless, balmy holidays blessed daylong by sun and accessible only by river.

Almost all initiation rites, however modest their aim, include the crossing of an obscure corridor; an excursion on the Evre is also comprised of such moments of unease in which the attention falters, the gaze is distracted. The river narrows, its characteristics become more defined; the water plants and even the reeds along the banks temporarily disappear. Along the now-steep riverbanks, the exposed roots of willows and ash cling precariously to clumps of earth that seem about to detach and slide off at any moment; warrens of water rats undermine many of the small, unstable cliffs. As the banks grow taller, nothing can be seen from the boat save the narrow waterway and the colors of the mud on each side, exposed tree roots, rats scurrying on wet patches of clay, and sometimes a delicate double line forming the obtuse angle of a grass snake's wake as it crosses the river: for a moment, a kind of foreboding hangs over the decaying banks so animated by the slight shifting of mud. Very quickly, though, the view changes again, widens: the unidentifiable silhouette of a floating object—the canopy in a Corpus Christi parade, or a lilliputian pagoda?—materializes, anchored permanently to the shore. The low hull that grazes the water, the perforated zinc roof that shades the square skiff, and the soapy streaks that sometimes lengthen over the Evre's surface hint at the boat's modest utilitarian use; however, this miniature facility resembles a public wash-shed about as much as a rowboat does a three-masted schooner. With only three spots for kneeling, it is destined for private use only, for washing the laundry of the nearby manor, whose weathervanes begin to appear across an expanse of English lawn. As a child, nothing would fill me with such utter delight as this misappropriation for private use of what I took to be a strictly public facility: I wouldn't have been any more stupefied if the lord of the manor owned a police station or a firehouse. Beyond this prestigious sign of feudal distinction, the entire course of the Evre seemed to bathe in a more rarefied, precious light. The last time I saw the wash-shed of La Gueriniere, a number of years ago now, the tops of the slender columns still held up the canopy, but it had half-sunk into a bank of clay—a pitiful sight, like the Vichy fleet scuttled in the shallows of Toulon: it seemed to me as if an entire fantasy of my youth had taken a nosedive into the mud.

A new bend of the Evre finally reveals an oblique view, in lost profile, of the manor: it remains, and always shall remain, fixed in my memory at around four o'clock in the afternoon.

Then a brick castle with corners of stone,
Its windows tinted with reddish colors,
Surrounded by vast parks, with a river
Bathing its feet, which flows amid flowers.

As long as I've known these lines by Nerval, a long time before *Les Chimères* (I must have been about twelve when I discovered them in a *Selected Works* distributed by my school library), one single image always comes to mind, which the others surround and enclose like a phylactery —the Guerinière manor, although the description is far from accurate. The park, which could hardly be called vast, is confined to a space between the hillside and the river, and the building is perhaps not ancient at all: hardly a château in the Mauges region dates back further than the last century (those that might have were all burned during the wars of the Vendée). But the river is there, the wide lawn is in front of the castle, and the silence, more ancient than the building, confers upon it its nobility; the hills recede for a moment from the river to showcase it, transforming the shrine of shallow foliage, in which the manor is set like a jewel, into a kind of theater box fashioned of greenery, walled in by the crest of slopes that separates it from the pastures, where it rests in a contemplative pose before the river that flows by calmly and luxuriously, the only spectacle capable of absorbing and enchanting it.

I now quietly recite Nerval's lines. Like the *Odelettes*, they're minor works and foretell nothing of what was yet to come—those miraculous, orphic sonnets he wrote late in life—but their spell on me is powerful; their tinny, frail sound is that of ancient keyboard instruments: the spinet, and especially the Elizabethan virginal, reminiscent of Vermeer's most mysterious work, a painting still vibrating from the liquid sonority of a key just released by the finger suspended in midair. At their call, a slight vapor, clear yet nocturnal, rises from the river and floats over the meadows, as in the passage from *Sylvie,* in which Adrienne sings, and now, effortlessly, a poem by Rimbaud links up with this memory to further fuel the rustic, naive white magic: "... the master's hand animates the meadow's keyboard; people play cards at the bottom of the pond, evocative mirror of queens and pretty girls; there are saints, veils, skeins of harmony, and legendary colorings against the setting sun." I am unable to resist these clusters of recollection, these adhesive elements that the impact of a cherished image hurriedly, anarchically condenses around itself; bizarre poetic stereotypes that, in our imagination, coagulate around a childhood vision in a jumble of fragments of poetry, painting, or music. Such fixed constellations (emblematic ties connecting the names, coats of arms, mottos, and colors of old, aristocratic families), as arbitrary as they first seem, play for the imagination the role of transformers of poetic energy: it is through connections that bind them together that the emotion born of a pastoral spectacle can extend freely across an artistic network—plastic, poetic, or musical—and traverse great distances without the least loss of energy. One of those concretions —or rather one of those interchanges, rich in intertwined images—formed itself in my mind, as far back as I can remember, around the manor and its clearing. Today, the nucleus it encloses has become as inaccessible for me as the original flower in the petrifying fountain.

On the left riverbank, before the castle comes into view, one passes the slope of a hill that plunges headlong into the Evre; its shadows seem to pour into the water like black ink, deepening the silence. There are no thickets beneath the dark yet uncrowded canopy; bare rocks, rounded like armor and resembling the sandstone formations of the little valleys of the Vosges Mountains, rise in tiers between the tree trunks. Not a single blade of grass pokes through the brown layer of pine needles and dried twigs that covers the ground: half a century ago, one could see beneath the tree branches two or three roughly hewn wooden tables, like those erected now in designated public picnic areas. Tepidly humanized by these charmless accessories, the site remains somber and heavily shaded. The half-light of the underbrush signals, menacingly: a bad place to stop, a caution evoked for me elsewhere by the infamous name of the woods called False Rests—a rendezvous for treachery, like the one that Hagen's horn turns from day to stormy dusk. Mount Frugy, before my eyes whenever I opened the window of a room I occupied in Quimper in 1938, whose steep, sturdy slopes I loved to look at, with its high, black line of beeches raised like an eyebrow above the still waters of the Odet (though already darkened by mountain shadow as well as looming war), later borrowed from that somber gorge the charm necessary to remembrance. So many landscapes that one by one, as the years passed, would invite me to linger, or move me, have, more than once, even when turning from light to dark, derived their suggestive power from signals addressed to them by those stations lining that liquid route beloved in childhood. The sudden bends in the Evre, the narrow field of vision procured by the river's plane once past the manor, made the appearance of successive sites seem, rather than merely a slow replacement of one view by another, slides brusquely beamed from a projector. Every image, at once an unalloyed element and a significant design, left its imprint on the blank slate of childhood. Passwords, still invalid, hermetic, and incomprehensible, like those so often encountered in Tales of the Round Table, inscribed themselves all along the way in the form of silent images that, despite their muteness, wished to speak; vividly, from start to finish, the sensation of taking a shortcut suffused the voyage.

The ear, no less than the eye, takes in the changes brought by nearly every bend in the river. Now that it is hemmed in by the hills, the faint noise of displaced water and thud of oars that accompany the boat's passage awaken echoes, grotto acoustics. Noises that travel over water—and that water, in turn, propels—have been familiar to me since childhood; as far back as I can remember, my father's boat—the long, flat, dark green vessel with its short bow, its *bascule* at the back that served as a fish tank, its middle seat pierced by a hole in which a mast could be inserted for a square sail—had been an almost daily sight in my life. It was moored on a bank of the Loire, thirty meters away from our front door; oars on my shoulder, oar locks in my hand, I would jump in it as easily as I would later hop on a bicycle. But the noises intersecting across the wide-open Loire—endless, monotonous small talk exchanged by the fishermen installed on opposing banks, wind rustling the leaves of the willow, a sound like foam hissing in the backwash of a wave, the clunk of the anchor dropped on floor-planks, the loud clap of little waves that join together to slap against the boat's blunt prow—awakened me even more to new sounds of the Evre itself, their singularity, their resounding solemnity, the hollow resonance that the valley, captivated by this ribbon of sleeping water, bestowed on them. Later on, the river that traverses the Argol countryside undoubtedly reminded me of the Evre's lead-like tint and abrupt darkening by shadows cast, like gathering storm clouds, from its banks. Whenever I traveled alone through these straits, I used to raise the oars for a moment or two and listen intensely, the boat continuing its roam, to an oppressive, vaguely ominous silence, as if, in the greenish half-light swallowing up the water, I had suddenly sailed past phantoms.

Just as all picturesque gorges have a cliff or overlook to which clings a banal legend, Devil's

Jump or Maiden's Leap, the Evre also has its site, not quite a historical monument, the highlight of an excursion on the river. It is called La Roche qui Boit, and I have always loved these words, perhaps even more than the site itself: they express my simple, vivid feeling of the Evre's bewitchment of its valley, of that immobile gorge bent like Narcissus over a poisonous pool, entranced by the smoke-tinted mirror whose simple reflection is itself an undertow, whose reflective power is also, simultaneously, its power to engulf. La Roche qui Boit is a slab of hardened shale that protrudes from the wooded cliff; it overhangs the Evre by about twelve meters before plunging straight into it and is reputed to have served as a diving board for one of the ladies of La Guerinière. Even on hot afternoons, an uncomfortable chill falls on one's shoulders as the boat drifts past the rock, under a high canopy of beech trees; the thought of diving into that water steeped with little brown turnip-shaped leaves is about as enticing as the prospect of a dive into the Tartarus. It is said that, at the foot of the rock, the depth of the river exactly equals the rock's height: though less frequented, fortunately, than Suicide Bridge, there seems no better place to drown oneself.

... In the midst of Saint-Sulpice's hazardous rock faces ... Suddenly, this disquieting scene the Evre has just skirted calls to mind the caption of an illustration in a cheap edition of Balzac's *Les Chouans*, in which I discovered a tale of suspense in an otherwise tense, distraught novel. Mademoiselle de Verneuil, facing the hillside of Fougères as night falls, an Afghan dagger tucked inside her belt, ascends the rock formations of Mount Nançon, which loom high above Saint-Sulpice's spire; her long riding skirt sweeps through the yellow grass, a muslin scarf—like those worn by indomitable Victorian ladies resolutely setting out to scale the Jungfrau or hunt tigers—tied to her boater flutters in the wind. What she hunts that uncertain night in her

strange outfit, stumbling and twisting her ankles on that path already traveled by the wood owl's cry, is her lover, the Marquis de Montauran, emissary of princes, and she still doesn't know if she'll denounce him or give herself to him. Could there be anything more distraught, I wonder each time I reopen the book, than this magnetized silhouette, completely oblivious of any definite end, who seems to draw her delight and sustenance solely from the inner turmoil that drives her onward?

I've never been able to pass through the town of Fougères without driving up its central slope to park my car briefly in front of Saint-Leonard's, the church that dominates it, with its bell tower that still looks, in Balzac's words, like a sugar loaf. High up on the hill, even in the heart of summer, the wind blows through its austere, nearly empty little streets. Once through the gate—whose rusty clang I know so well—that leads to the gravel paths and terrace of the lovely public gardens, I suddenly find myself in the center of a book, as if sent by magic into the heart of a diamond, where all facets conspire to capture the light and create a dazzling surface. To the right are the scattered stone blocks of Papegaut, the beheaded tower, where the house rented by Corentin for Marie de Verneuil once stood— here are the cliffs scaled by the Chouans from Marche-à-Terre in the grandiose finale of that last night, when the population of the entire town and countryside, armed and silently waiting, seems to come alive in the darkness like an erratic compass, and oscillates around a fire that burns steadily high up in the lovers' room. Here is the Queen's stairway, down which Marie, a gowned torrent, rushes to look for Gars. Here is the mass of the enormous castle straddling its petrified foundation of shale blocks; the rocks of Saint-Sulpice, where the deadly smoke will rise and on which the top of the church's spire is still nestled; and the green meadows of Mount Nançon, in which the adventuress crosses the old bridge. Behind me, to the left, hidden for a moment by the shoulder of the hill, are the Valley of Gibarry, the Nest of Fangs, and Galope-Chopine's blood-soaked cottage—a few steps to the right, the guardpost Hulot situated right up against the church. Almost directly before me—and now the attention sharpens, the eye strains to calculate the exact distance—is the abrupt ledge of Mount Nançon's other face. It is here, without a doubt, that Marie, out walking, suddenly recognized Gars and the officers of his royal infantry across the river; it is the very same rock, facing the Promenade, from which Madame du Gua aimed so carefully at the rival who stood exactly where I am standing now; that shot, fired two centuries ago, is about to resound; the sleeping ghosts arise, beckoned by the magic of the text: everything begins again, *everything is real*; nothing more than a rifle's range. And now the gaze goes back to scrutinize "the hazardous rock faces of

Saint-Sulpice," where a tall, thin silhouette still glimmers in the gathering dusk, vanishes, then reappears intermittently like a lighted torch: all the book's brushfires burn inside her, accompanying her flight. Burning phantom—tender cyclone—queen of disguises in a fantastic, pastoral opera, may your night never end!—mad night in which you search for your lover in a maze of hedges, your veil waving, the sharp curved dagger at your side, long train of your dress—*fabulously elegant*—hurtling wooden fences. May your marvelous extravagance—for a long time, forever!—set aflame, one by one, each page of that enchanted book.

I haven't left the Evre. But that image that suddenly appears at an outcropping of rocks, an image of a human will-o'-the-wisp fluttering over the moonlit earth—an image so immediately seductive that I can almost hear the supernatural silence and feel the dread left in the wake of its fickle trajectory—keeps me spellbound: it calls forth a more blurred, more perplexing image: where could it be, in what even more distant night does a half-crazed woman with disheveled hair keep on waving a torch in my memory, trying to anchor this fleeting image to a place, to a name that time has not been able to completely erase? The night bursts and the emblematic name resurfaces: this indistinct, seductive ghost about to disappear forever, whom the recollection of Marie de Verneuil brings back to the surface inch by inch as if from the bottom of a well, is the Wandering Flame, who hovers at night in the Indian plateau of Ripore over a man attached to the mouth of a cannon, in the final scene of one of Jules Verne's strangest novels: *The House of Steam*.

Strange how the liquid element in this wildly associative daydream set off by still waters that reflect the steep face of La Roche qui Boit has been slowly replaced by fire. Not that its course has betrayed the original element. But a daydream is not always from beginning to end bound to matter, since it (like most daydreams, no doubt) is under the spell, as Gaston Bachelard believes, of some more elemental genie who might awaken *inside* the matter, like a dark heart. The mesmerizing daydream—most exclusive, most haunting of them all—undoubtedly follows a descending route, since a certain kind of weight pulls it toward those frontier regions where the spirit allows itself to become caught up in the world, almost integrated into one of its realms. But there exists another less common daydream, one tied to other privileges and almost always a sign of a feeling of freedom, and often, too, of the overwhelming ubiquity associated with the most beautiful dreams of flying: a daydream of ascension, its goal neither to reach some final, distinct stage nor to find refuge in the security of an element, but rather to search for the total freedom of association that leaves the play of images and signification forever open-ended: its exclusive climate is speed, and its favorite trajectory the short-cut. An unreal lightness, a certain sensation of happiness, fills the spirit as soon as one has embarked, as if flying trapezes with miraculously synchronized oscillations, set against an infinite background, danced along every airy path. Such a daydream is most likely to occur only at rare moments, launched and carried along by the flow of energy released when memory reanimates objects or landscapes of previously violent, emotional tonality, as if that memory, in reviving them, had suddenly endowed them with a magical power of fission. Proust's name is linked to the resurrection of an abolished fragment by means of a reunion with an object. But memory's sudden release of the genie held captive inside matter, like a spirit bottled by an evil witch, is much more often for me both generator and principle of a happy, feverish *fugue* than the quietism of a Proustian illumination. Resparked, the precious images kept so long in darkness—all of them—ignite and set each other ablaze; a flaming line zig-zags across a dozing world and sows it with light as it travels the secret fissures—an experience, a reading, a decisive encounter that prompts another—that have, year after year, marked it with my initials. The virtue of genuine contact with something that had at one time captivated me is that it awakens, reanimates, and binds with streaks of lightning everything I have ever loved.

How odd that—reflecting on the significance and, moreover, on the montage of this interior film that resurrected impressions of the Evre have set in motion—I return again to Poe, this time not to the poet of *Fairyland* or *The Domain of Arnheim,* but to the analyst of *The Murders in the Rue Morgue.* No matter that Poe—something that annoys me—speaks of chess with obvious incompetence, the excessively long prologue (a hallmark of his works) that opens this prototypical detective novel has intrigued me since I first opened the book. The night at Mr. Dupin's—

a night Poe first began to illuminate when I was quite young: I must have been about twelve or thirteen—has never paled in comparison to Valéry's *Evening with Mr. Teste*. The chevalier Auguste Dupin already *is* a Mr. Teste, barely tarnished by his periodic run-ins with the police, but a Mr. Teste who would furnish his own proofs, and testify, by working them out, to a possession of power and spirit that Valéry only *credits* his own Mr. Teste as having—an entrancing, disturbing image that has relentlessly pursued me since I first came across it. I could never imagine Dupin dressed in any other costume than the one he wore while searching for the purloined letter: to me he will always be a man with dark glasses and a vacant, terribly modern, inscrutable face that deflects our stare, a face that is nothing more than a portal opening onto circuits more amazing than those of a computer.

Just for the record: while the narrator and Dupin are walking side by side on the dark streets of

Paris, an observation made by Dupin after an extended period of silence so resembles the narrator's own unspoken thought that he realizes Dupin, thanks to his flawless interpretation of the sequence of images in the narrator's mind, has followed the projection of the narrator's "interior film" from start to finish. This discovery panics the narrator, and he protests such seemingly heretical piracy (in 1975, we know better). My own reaction is less straightforward. This way of reading the subtlest imaginary connections, those generated, for example, in poetry (I am immediately reminded of tactics elaborated and employed by contemporary criticism), worries me at times, as if it revealed a quasi-religious domain of the forbidden. But this hostile reaction also has its counterpart. What has captivated me while playing chess are those theoreticians like Steinitz and Rubinstein for whom any opening error by the opponent is acceptable, since it causes a small break in that closed, limited realm of mental activity—the lifting of the last remaining veils, the revelation of ultimate secrets. These remarkable heroes of abstraction, loners whose fanaticism no one comprehends, destined for the sorest of solitudes, are caught early on in merciless combat, in a race between famine and the search for some marginally interesting, frivolous absolute. Between my partiality, in this regard, for adventurers playing with high stakes, for whom everything aside from the object of their particular quest is transparent right from the start (like the accidental passenger in *The Manuscript Found in a Bottle,* whom the explorers boarding the phantom ship look at, suggestively, without really seeing), between that instinctive preference and the uneasiness caused me by the current spectacle of so many hands held out not to poetry (which barely interests them) but only to an enigmatic *key* to poetry—between each of these there is a contradiction I recognize but have trouble solving. In other words, for me penetrating the secrets of language would never liberate those secrets of poetry. For half a century now we've been told that poetry doesn't depend on any outside support, and thus it has been reduced to merely an interrelation of its mechanisms. It is not that this desire to find a total solution seems retrograde, but rather that restricting the field confines research to the medium, not irreplaceable, of language. In every attempt to elucidate the poetic phenomenon and the dispute between humankind and the world that nourishes it (the world considered an objective), the controversial ground in which poetry roots itself cannot even for a moment figure as an excluded third party. And it is remarkable that, until now, there has been a sort of equilibrium between the development of the means of analysis and the continuous expansion of the terrain traveled by poetry written in the last century, even more so by poetry written in ours. It comes as no surprise that the analytical methods critics presently boast of hardly exceed, comparatively (if, in fact, they compare at all), those methods employed by critics disabled by conditions prevailing in earlier times—three centuries ago, for example—when the extreme surveillance under which works were conceived and an enforced code of poetics exercised a stranglehold.

Only Chinese painting (Song Dynasty landscapes in particular) has been haunted by the humble theme of a solitary rowboat moving through a wooded gorge. Clearly the great charm of such an image derives from the contrast between the sheer physical effort evoked by the steep slopes and the level, incredible ease of the river flowing eternally between peaks: the jubilant feeling born, in the dreamer's consciousness, of the discovery of an effortless solution to contradictions here becomes fixed in reality. Vaulted tree branches beneath which one glides along, branches of rock-loving pines that hang in angles over the water in Chinese drawings, intensify the feeling of calm intoxication and can give way, in a moment—with the whimsy of a ribbon of water ringed by precipices—to a protected intimacy, the alluring fancy of canopies of trees cradling a canal that runs straight into the horizon. Eyes closed, one abandons oneself to the water which, unfailingly, cuts a passage; no excursion is more entrancing than the one in which the sensation of well-being, as one is carried along by a current, is coupled with the magical security of Ariadne's thread. And so, for many a long minute, the boat moves forward in blue-green silence; the sun and the cliffs stifle all but the slightest breaths of air. Midway along an excursion on the Evre, silent moments like these begin to resemble, in my memory, a long pause in music, a mute chord; this hush—an erect, still finger held to the lips, semi-materialized in the hollow of these phantom-filled straights—could only have been imposed by a local deity.

I react to capricious accidents of light and

shadow with a feeling of joy and warmth, and, perhaps even more, with a vague sense of joy yet to come, a feeling inseparable from what I call, for want of a better expression, *a belated beautifying*. For example, the late afternoon of a long day of constant rain is beautified by a yellow ray of miraculous limpidity that emerges from behind a cover of breaking clouds (the damp, Nordic skies of Ruysdael); from time to time, I find this twilight beautification of the horizon (more luminous, warmer) at the Louvre in *Virgin with Rabbit*—a little Titian painting that captivates me. Such a distinctive feeling of warmth and comfort, perhaps more invigorating for me than for others, is like a charged religious image, imprinted in us ages ago, where a foreshadowed life can only reveal itself in all its glory on the other side of the "obscure corridor," valley of darkness, or place of exile. The image of daytime turning to dusk, which often represents life's flow, might also optimistically suggest a possible halting of decline and perhaps even an inversion of the flow of time, if it is presented to our innermost sense by this rejuvenation of afternoon sun. In any case, I'm almost certain that a heightened memory inside us, sensitized by nature to signals beyond the quotidian that regulates our lives, vouches for the reality of these vague, yet passionate, promises constantly made to us by time, weather, and season. The already setting sun, hidden while traversing these narrow waters, reappears now in full force; where it touches the liquid surface, this surface, only moments ago an unreassuring indicator of the river's depth, appears almost opaque in the rays, as if covered again by a thin film of dust. Sunlight sprays in bursts across the branches and boughs of ash and willow trees; as if accompanied by the opening of parasols, one glides again across a tender and airy summer landscape flying the colors of "fine weather prevailing."

On each side of the river in the west between Bas-Maine and Finistère is a landscape multiplied obsessively: not quite a gorge, but rather a narrow, steeply banked valley full of rock outcroppings, choking, anemic humus, and nothing to which a forest might cling—nothing but clumps of dry heather, thickets of dwarf chestnut, ferns on shadowy slopes, and, especially during the flowering season, two shades of yellow (subtly different, but both incurably tinged with sadness): saffron-tinted broom and gorse grass the color of wasps. The former is fresher, with a more sulphury complexion, and better suited to springtime's acid spectrum; the latter, more mature, muted and concentrated like old wine, glimmers on the green-black bushes like a brushfire on dry needles. I have always loved genuinely (though joylessly) these slopes splashed with lifeless yellow and pierced by lichen-infested granite slabs (a widowed spring, reminiscent of late fall, already the color of autumn berries)—a sad, flowerless yellow I find a much better match for the plaintive, frail brooding of the shepherd's flute in *Tristan* than any heathery hue. One afternoon I set off on foot from Tréhorenteuc, a sordid hamlet with dung-encrusted roads—one of those dead-end places stuck in the mud of deep Brittany, beyond which there could be nothing but ruts and shrubs, solitude, silence, and rain. Almost as soon as I started walking down the muddy path, the weather began to clear, which, in Brittany, means the freeing up of a delicately blue, fresh corner of the sky; the path, climbing among rocks and tufts of boxwood, became dry and pleasant to follow; it led across stands of scrub oak, fern-covered hills, clearings paved with rounded rocks that seemed arranged for some kind of megalith. To the right, beyond stands of holm oak and young pine, the view was clearing: through the sunbeams and cloud shadow that animated it, I embraced in one look the landscape I'd set out to find at the end of these forsaken paths, spurred on solely by the magic of a name.

Le Val sans Retour looks nothing like what one might imagine: neither the narrow cleft, like a saber slash, which provides access to an infamous gorge nor the somber green of lowlands choked by trees whose branches rain sleep like those of the manzanilla. It is only a rather deep ravine, wide open on both sides, that has dug itself a winding swath through a high plateau of fallow land and moors; to the west extends the forest of Paimpont, whose farthest treetops can be made out at view's end and look like the scattered flags of some rear guard retreating behind the horizon. From the top of the hill, the valley's panorama, the absolute leveling of the line of the horizon, seizes the eye—a worn-down base, a planed block into which is sunk the valley's closed-in, finger-like enclave with its short tributary ravines arranged like the veins of a leaf. The rocky skeletal structure surfaces at each point on the slopes as well-worn, flattened, rounded, lichen-encrusted rocks of a dull white hue, a

color that haunts Brittany. A rough, sparse vegetation occupies all the intervals: trails of dry rush,
low, darker green brushlands of broom and gorse
spread out like scabrous sheets, misplaced oaks,
stands of dwarf fir cascading in black trails to the
bottom of the ravine. Up where the slopes reach
the plateau, as soon as their angles diminish,
thickets of stunted chestnut trees, roots exposed,
cling to everything stiff as stubble on a shaved
neck; in winter, a jumble of birches stripped of all
but the tiniest twigs fills the bottom of the ravine
with the soft gray of mouse down so dense it's
mistaken for mounting fog.

There is nothing—besides irregular shades
of green that stain it no matter which season
—to attract the eye to this landscape of self-
perpetuating moors that stretches ad nauseam to
the west. And yet, how can one explain why the
eye is drawn, lingers, practically weds itself to the
unchanging hollow groove, which for me is like
an afternoon sky covered with clouds whose

indeterminately wandering shadows scale the slopes again in order to be suddenly swallowed by the horizon's heavy line? The title of a Noël Delvaux story occurs to me, which I like because it suggests the freedom associated with crossing over into certain dormant fringes of the Earth: *At the Margins of Known Land.* The idea of even a small stretch of terrestrial space where a magic wand has suspended the flow of time, frozen life, withered the vegetation, stopped gestures in midair, holds great sway over the imagination, beyond even the domain of fairy tales; in fact, this power derives from the fact that, in this case, fiction is fully authorized by experience and if we interrogate deepest memory, it will tell us that we have seen fairytale castles and cursed lands at least once, on some detour in life. The gaze comes back to linger deep in the cloistered valley then wanders along the deserted slopes: not a single trace of man's presence: not a single house, field, path—not even a trace of smoke. Torpor descends from the covered sky—no sound of running springs, no birdsong. It is not so much the imprint of a fabled past that weighs on the dead valley like an occluded threat, but rather a feeling of total distraction from quotidian existence. Here nothing has stirred; like the shadows of clouds, passing epochs have left no trace: more than the impact of legend, what bewitches this abandoned valley, this vacant, ever-fallow terrain, is the sensation that the powerful magic that still reigns here, with all its might, is the undoing of Time. Whenever I encounter, in these western moors, barren ravines colored with, but never brightened by, the embalmed yellow of gorse grass, I find it hard not to love them: it seems I could wander there all day long: ravines of La Hague, which tumble down, inside the humid hollow of their swollen, round slopes, like a furrow between breasts, toward a lilac-colored sea; heather-covered ravines in the Limousin Mountains, filled with the tinkling of water and cowbells, spotted with the pink and vibrant yellow of oriental carpets spread out for drying on the rocks of a river ford. What I search for in these amnesiac moors is not the trace of something fabulous, but merely life, life on these pathless, ageless lands, freeing itself from points of reference and anchorage to become anonymous, clouded, legendary: unbeknownst to him, Ossian's minstrel becomes a poet here. Where the path, barrier, and fence have reached the end, where the bridle and rein failed in their efforts to subjugate, they disappeared from the conscious mind: for me, the sense of this land's deep freedom can never be entirely separated from the notion of *le terrain vague.*

Meanwhile, the hillside slopes level off, and the sun, though withdrawing, floods the entire valley again with an even yellower light, like ripening fruit, introducing into the now straightforward course of the journey a purely theatrical move: the return to calm after the culmination of a dramatic scene. One more bend in the river, and the end of the navigable stretch appears, revealing some of the most pleasant and picturesque details a water mill could offer: the narrow, still river with its palisades of reeds—here in the form of decorative bulrushes with tall, lead-tipped spikes; the partially opened water lilies in the dark shadow of the riverbank; the building at water's edge, overgrown with ivy, buried in the half-light of the trees; the water cascading, in vivid, silvery arcs, like jumping trout, over the sides of the dam and into the fresh pandemonium below. Where the downstream dam is silent between banks of black weeds and drowning in poisonous shadows cast from the steep banks, the upstream dam is joyous and sunbathed; the eye still contentedly follows without any regret the curve of the valley that beckons beyond the dam and stops, fully satisfied, in front of this symbolic barrier cleared by a jumping fish.

Time now to turn around and go back, after

having anchored the boat in a clearing among the reeds and stretched out for a moment on a grassy bank. The sun still valiantly warms the little valley; not even a hint of breeze, but a band of cool air already stretches out at the foot of each tree along the riverside, distinct as shadow. I've often heard singing in the boats coming back from Coulènes; like water smoothing out over the crest of a dam, what poured out of that singing was surplus tranquility—only that which finally overflowed, without violence, from the intake of a cloudless day. The returning voices, which evening isolates and makes fluid, resonate in the echo of La Roche qui Boit; the square tower of the chapel at last comes into view above the reedbeds: the bronze bell's languid sounding of the hour carries closer than expected and seems to broaden over the water, then dies out slowly, like the ripples made by a stone tossed into a pond. It is only from here, framed by feathery reed bouquets reflected on the trembling waters and broken up like a mosaic by leaves of water chestnuts and water lilies, that this ugly pilgrims' building somehow deserves one's gaze and merits the secret name I keep for it in my memory, a name I stole from a poor village in La Brière: Chapelle-des-Marais. For me a sensation of security has always come from this name and image, and the reason for this is hard to discern: could it be that —since for me, *marshland* represents an endlessly germinating, maternal nature, more so even than the earth or the sea—the tower provides equilibrium as a more virile guardian who, in sentry-like vigil, rallies and reassures something inside of me that life's pressures keep fraught with feelings of anxiety?

The boat has been moored again at the riverbank; the familiar click of the padlock is like the clasp of a necklace now closed at day's end, a day distinct from other days. Present and past inextricably intertwine in the parade of images of this excursion I've made many times, and which, even now, nothing could prevent me from making again. Nothing could have really changed along the Evre, except perhaps the cutting of a few stands of reeds, the plundering of green colonies of water chestnuts, and, I wager, the final collapse of the enigmatic wash-shed. Nothing, or almost nothing, has changed in the hamlet of Marillais, which I cross nearly every week in summer—a new garage has sprung up beside the road; the cavernous, shadowy shop where, for nearly half a century, an old woman in a tall starched cap sold flatbreads to the pilgrims has closed its shutters. What stops me the moment I think of setting out again on the narrow, still river is not the fear of dispelling the charm of memories. Rather, it's the impossibility of reanimating a dream, or at least of finding again, while daydreaming, its sourceless light, of feeling again its rhythm which, although devoid of any notion of speed, never ceases to change. The domains of Arnheim *do* exist, and each of us has encountered them at least once—but the mysterious current that seizes and propels the crescent-shaped boat is the pulsing of youthful blood, a continuous palpitation of the future. The images that unfold along every initiatory journey enigmatically recall a destined encounter, an encounter they both foretell and later incarnate; the potent charm of these magic forays, such as my own on the Evre, derives its strength from the fact that all of them are, in their own way, "paths of life," occult representations of future climates and stages. Not all the qualities I assign to the Evre are imagined, and perhaps I'll find them again, intact, along this retrospective journey I sometimes consider taking again. But everything colored like dream is, by its nature, prophetic, facing forward, and the charms that once opened roads for me can no longer have any virtue or vigor: these images— each of them—can no longer summon me anywhere, and I no longer have time to encounter anything the Evre might still wish to show me.